# Freddy's Day at the Races

Story by Susan Chalker Browne

Illustrations by HildaRose

**Freddy** woke up early and raced into the kitchen.

"It's Regatta Day!" announced the woman on the radio in a cheerful voice.

"All stores and businesses are closed. The weather forecast is sunny and warm with hardly any wind. A wonderful day for the races!"

So Freddy gobbled his egg, brushed his teeth and dressed in his pirate's suit. First he pulled on his black and red striped pants. Then he buttoned his white shirt and over that went a black vest with shiny red trim. He fixed an eye patch over one eye, fit a gold earring in one ear and finished off with a large pirate's hat.

Then he and his mom drove down to the pond.

ROYAL ST. JOHN'S REGATTA

A 'regatta' is a series of boat races.

Sunshine sparkled on the still waters of Quidi Vidi Lake. People swarmed like bees, their t-shirts and hats resembling bright bits of confetti. Freddy and his mom jumped from the car and pushed their way into the crush. Children shrieked, old men stood nodding their heads, and the smell of French fries and vinegar drifted on the warm breeze. Suddenly a loud crack snapped through the air.

ROYAL ST. JOHN'S REGATTA

The Royal St. John's Regatta is the oldest organized sporting event in North America.

"That's the gun to start the first race!" cried Freddy's mom.
"See all the rowers? Look at those racing shells go!"
But when she turned toward Freddy, he was gone.
Off in the distance, a black pirate's hat disappeared
into the crowd.

ROYAL ST. JOHN'S REGATTA

The first organized Regatta
was held in 1818 in
St. John's Harbour.

Down by the water's edge, Freddy raced by
the cotton candy stand.

"Cotton candy, sticky and sweet!" called out a boy
in a sideways baseball cap. "Seventy-five cents for one!"

Freddy grinned and thought about the sweet taste
of cotton candy on his tongue, but didn't stop at all.

ROYAL ST. JOHN'S REGATTA

Regatta Day draws
fifty thousand people to
Quidi Vidi Lake each year.

A few seconds later Freddy's mom came huffing by, red-faced and all out of breath. "Have you seen a small pirate?" she asked the boy in the sideways cap. "Wearing black and red striped pants?"

"Yes ma'am, I have," replied the boy, as he swirled up a fluffy blue cloud. "He went that way." And he pointed toward a black pirate's hat disappearing into the crowd.

ROYAL ST. JOHN'S REGATTA

The Regatta is held on the first Wednesday of August, if the weather permits. Otherwise, it's held the next suitable day.

Down by the water's edge, Freddy rushed by
the big Titanic Slide.

"Take a slide on a sinking ship!" called out a woman
in pink polka dot pants. "A toonie for a turn!"

Freddy grinned and thought about whooshing down
the slide, but didn't stop at all.

A few seconds later Freddy's mom came huffing by, red-faced and all out of breath. "Have you seen a small pirate?" she asked the woman in the polka dot pants. "Wearing a gold earring in one ear?"

"Yes ma'am, I have," replied the woman, as she counted the coins in her hand. "He went that way." And she pointed toward a black pirate's hat disappearing into the crowd.

ROYAL ST. JOHN'S REGATTA

In 1978, to accommodate the visit of Queen Elizabeth II and Prince Phillip, the Regatta was held a week early.

Down by the water's edge, Freddy darted by a booth full of stuffed monkeys and giraffes.

"Two for a quarter, ten for a dollar!" called out a man with a shiny bald head. "You can't win if you're not in!"

Freddy grinned and thought about winning the enormous spotted giraffe, but didn't stop at all.

ROYAL ST. JOHN'S REGATTA
The St. John's Regatta was renamed the Royal St. John's Regatta in 1993, an honour given by Queen Elizabeth II.

TWO·25¢
ten·$1

A few seconds later Freddy's mom came huffing by, red-faced and all out of breath. "Have you seen a small pirate?" she asked the man with the bald head. "Wearing a black patch over one eye?"

"Yes ma'am, I have," replied the man, as he tore off a long strip of tickets. "He went that way." And he pointed toward a black pirate's hat disappearing into the crowd.

ROYAL ST. JOHN'S REGATTA
In 1877 a Placentia crew carried their boat 145 km to the Regatta, rowed the fastest time, then hiked home again.

Down by the water's edge, Freddy dashed by the covered bandstand. Cheerful marching music boomed from trumpets and trombones.

"Enjoy the show!" called out the conductor, as she waved her baton in the air. "What's Regatta Day without the band?"

Freddy grinned and thought about dancing to the boom-boom of the drum, but didn't stop at all.

ROYAL ST. JOHN'S REGATTA

Three men drowned in the 1884 Regatta when their boat, the *Terra Nova*, capsized.

A few seconds later Freddy's mom came huffing by, red-faced and all out of breath. "Have you seen a small pirate?" she asked the conductor, shouting over the trumpets and trombones. "Wearing a vest with shiny red trim?"

"Yes, ma'am, I have," yelled back the conductor, cupping her hands to her face. "He went that way." And she pointed her baton toward a black pirate's hat disappearing into the crowd.

ROYAL ST. JOHN'S REGATTA

There was no Regatta in 1892 because of the Great Fire. People whose homes had burned were camped around the pond.

Down by the water's edge, Freddy ran and ran and ran.
Past the hot dog booth and the sweet smell of roasting
wieners. Past moms and dads pushing baby strollers,
wearing big wide hats and sipping cool drinks. He leaped
over mud puddles and scooted between laughing teenagers.
The hot sun prickled his skin and the roar of the crowd
pounded in his ears.

Finally Freddy stopped.

ROYAL ST. JOHN'S REGATTA

In 1901 the crew from Outer
Cove set a course record which
remained unbroken for 80 years.

A few seconds later Freddy's mom came huffing by, red-faced and all out of breath.

"What are you doing, Freddy?" she cried, her eyes blazing. "Why are you running away?"

Freddy looked puzzled. "I wasn't running away, I was racing—like the rowers," he said, grinning. "Racing to the pirate's ship. Look!"

Behind Freddy an enormous pirate's ship rocked and rolled on the grassy bank. Fierce black cannons pointed straight out and white sails ballooned in the breeze. On the ship's deck, children and parents screamed with delight as they rode imaginary waves. At the very tip top of the tallest mast, a pirate's flag flapped in the wind.

"See that flag," said Freddy, proudly. "I followed it all the way here. As soon as we parked the car, I saw it!"

ROYAL ST. JOHN'S REGATTA
The Regatta was cancelled from 1915-1918 because of World War I.

Then Freddy's mom smiled and all her anger melted away. "You're a true pirate," she laughed, hugging Freddy closely.

"Shiver me timbers!" shouted the big, burly pirate who stood on the gangplank and scowled at everyone waiting in line. "A toonie to sail the seven seas!" The scary pirate wore black and red striped pants, a patch over his eye and a gold earring in one ear. Suddenly he noticed Freddy and his face broke into a wide smile.

"Ahoy, landlubbers! What have we here? Aye, 'tis a tiny buccaneer!" Then he turned toward the people waiting and made an announcement. "The little matey rides for free!" he proclaimed in a jolly voice. "Would he and his mom please step to the front of the line?"

ROYAL ST. JOHN'S REGATTA
A non-competitive race was held for women in 1856. The first official Ladies Race was in 1949.

Freddy and his mom gasped with delight as they skipped up the gangplank. A few seconds later they were strapped into their seats. Before them the oval pond reflected the brilliant blue of the sky. Then the pirate ship lurched into life and Freddy felt his stomach drop.

"We're sailing the high seas," he whispered excitedly to his mom, "searching for pirate gold!"

The gigantic ship pitched and plunged. Swooped and shook. Rattled and rolled. Freddy and his mom laughed and shrieked and hung on tightly. The sunlight sparkled, the seagulls soared—and the crowd roared as the thin boats raced up the pond.

ROYAL ST. JOHN'S REGATTA

The 'Greasy Pole' was once a popular Regatta game. Players tried to walk a greased pole suspended over the water.

©2008, Susan Chalker Browne

**Canada Council** **Conseil des Arts**
**for the Arts** **du Canada**

Newfoundland
Labrador

We gratefully acknowledge the financial support of
The Canada Council for the Arts, the Government
of Canada through the Book Publishing Industry
Development Program (BPIDP), and the Government of
Newfoundland and Labrador through the Department
of Tourism, Culture and Recreation for our publishing
program.

Illustrations ©2008, Kathy (HildaRose) Kaulbach
Design and layout by Kathy Kaulbach

Published by

**Tuckamore Books**
a Creative Publishers imprint

A Transcontinental Inc. associated company
P.O. Box 8660, Station A
St. John's, Newfoundland A1B 3T7

Printed in Canada by: Transcontinental Inc.

**Library and Archives Canada Cataloguing in Publication**

Browne, Susan Chalker, 1958-
Freddy's day at the races / written by Susan Chalker Browne;
illustrated by HildaRose.

ISBN 978-1-897174-36-4

I. Rose, Hilda, 1955-  II. Title.
PS8553.R691F74 2008    jC813'.6
C2008-903674-3